ONE SNOWY NIGHT

First published in hardback in Great Britain
by William Collins Sons & Co Ltd in 1989
First published in paperback by Picture Lions in 1991
New edition reissued in 1992
This edition published by Collins Picture Books in 2003

13 15 17 19 20 18 16 14

ISBN-13: 978-0-00-714693-2

Picture Lions and Collins Picture Books are imprints of the Children's Division,
part of HarperCollins Publishers Ltd.

Text and illustrations copyright © Nick Butterworth 1989

Visit our website at: www.harpercollins.co.uk

Printed in China by South China Printing Co.Ltd

A TALE FROM PERCY'S PARK

ONE SNOWY NIGHT

NICK BUTTERWORTH

HarperCollins *Children's Books*

It's cold in the park in winter. But Percy the park keeper doesn't mind.

He puts on his warm coat and his big scarf and wears two pairs of woolly socks inside his wellington boots.

Percy likes to be out in the fresh air.

In the middle of the park there is a little hut. This is where Percy lives.

When it gets too cold to be outside, Percy goes into his hut where it's cosy and warm.

T he animals who live in the park all know
Percy's hut. Every day he shares his lunch
with them.

One winter's night it was so cold it began to snow. Great big snowflakes fell past the window of Percy's hut.

"Brr," said Percy. "I think I'll need an extra blanket tonight."

He made himself some hot cocoa and got ready for bed.

Suddenly, Percy heard a tapping sound. There was somebody at the door.

"Now who can that be at this time of night?" thought Percy. He went to the door and looked out.

There on the step was a squirrel. It looked very cold and miserable.

"I can't get to sleep, Percy," said the squirrel. "My bed is full of snow."

"Oh dear," said Percy. "Never mind, I've got plenty of room for two."

The squirrel snuggled down next to Percy
and soon began to feel warm.

Knock! Knock! It was the door again.

"Now who can that be?"
thought Percy.

It was a fox! He looked very cold and hungry. "Can I come in, too?" he asked.

P ercy scratched his head and thought for a minute.

"Well, if you promise to behave," he said.

"I promise," said the fox, and he squeezed into bed next to all the other animals.

Bump! Oops! The squirrel fell out.

"Who did that?" asked the squirrel crossly.

The animals looked frightened and the mice all started to squeak at once.

"Oh dear!"

"What can it be?"

"It might be a monster!"

"With fierce claws!"

"And sharp teeth!"

The noise grew louder and louder. Then, one of the floorboards began to move.

"Look out! It's coming up through the floor!"

Suddenly, there was a loud creak.

"Help!" cried the animals and they all ran to hide.

But Percy wasn't frightened. He started to chuckle. Then he laughed out loud.

A small, dark head was sticking up through the floorboards.

"This isn't a monster," said Percy. "It's a mole!"

"I'm sorry to burst in like this," said the mole. "I knocked on the door but nobody heard me."

Percy helped the mole up through the hole in the floor, sat him on his hot water bottle to get warm and put the floorboard back.

"It's all right everyone," he called. "You can come out now."

But nobody moved. Nobody stirred. Nobody wanted to come out.

The squirrel was tucked away in the pocket of Percy's dressing gown.

The hedgehog was in his coat.

The fox…

the rabbits…

the badger…

and the ducks were all safely hidden away.

The mice had even squeezed themselves into Percy's slippers!

Everyone had found a cosy bed.

"Well I never!" said Percy.

P ercy yawned and snuggled down in his own bed once again.

"That's better. Now I've got plenty of room," he said. "And a little to spare…

…for a mole!"

"I was born in London in 1946 and grew up in a sweet shop in Essex. For several years I worked as a graphic designer, but in 1980 I decided to concentrate on writing and illustrating books for children.

My wife, Annette, and I have two grown-up children, Ben and Amanda, and we have put down roots in Suffolk.

I haven't recently counted how many books there are with my name on the cover but Percy the Park Keeper accounts for a good many of them. I'm reliably informed that they have sold more than four million copies worldwide. Hooray!

I didn't realise this when I invented Percy, but I can now see that he's very like my mum's dad, my grandpa. Here's a picture of him giving a ride to my mum and my brother, Mike, in his old home-made wheelbarrow!"

Nick Butterworth has presented children's stories on television, worked on a strip for *Sunday Express Magazine* and worked for various major graphic design companies. Among his books published by HarperCollins are *Thud!*, *QPootle5* and *Jingle Bells*, but he is best-known for his stories about Percy the Park Keeper. There are now more than 30 books about Percy, who features on video, audio tape and CD, as well as having his own television series.

Percy the Park Keeper stories can be ordered at:
www.harpercollins.co.uk